S0-AEY-153

Disney Girls

Beauty's Revenge

Gabrielle Charbonnet

Disney PRESS

NEW YORK

Copyright © 1999 by Disney Enterprises, Inc.

All rights reserved. No part of this book may be reproduced or
transmitted in any form or by any means, electronic or mechanical,
including photocopying, recording, or by any information storage and
retrieval system, without written permission from the publisher. For
information address Disney Press, 114 Fifth Avenue, New York,
New York 10011-5690.

Printed in the United States of America.

First Edition

1   3   5   7   9   10   8   6   4   2

The text of this book is set in 15-point Adobe Garamond.

Library of Congress Catalog Card Number: 98-88038

ISBN: 0-7868-4272-5

For more Disney Press fun, visit www.disneybooks.com

Contents

Chapter One

My Worst Nightmare

"No," I whispered in horror. The blood drained from my face, and for a moment I felt almost dizzy. "Tell me you're kidding."

"Of course I'm not kidding," my mom said briskly. "It's the perfect solution. This way, Delia and Tom can still go to Canada. Otto doesn't have to go to a kennel, and you've already had chicken pox. So it's no problem."

I sat down hard on a kitchen chair. No problem? No *problem*? That's how my mom described the worst thing that could ever possibly happen to me?

1

I'm sorry. Are you totally lost? Sometimes I just start off in the middle of things. Anyway, I'm Isabelle Beaumont. I'm in fourth grade at Orlando Elementary in, you guessed it, Orlando, Florida. I live with my mom and dad in an Orlando suburb called Willow Hill. Next door to us live the McIlhennys: Mr. and Mrs. McIlhenny, their disgusting son, Kenny, and Kenny's equally disgusting dog, Otto.

What I was bummed about was the fact that the McIlhennys were about to go to Canada for ten days because Kenny's mom had a business trip, and Kenny's dad was going along just for fun. Until today, Kenny was supposed to go with them. Frankly, I had been thrilled at the idea of getting rid of him for ten days. He's in my class at school, plus he lives next door, and I just get more Kenny than any one person should have to bear.

Now, only hours before I had expected to be Kenny-free, my mom was dropping a bomb on my world.

"Mom," I tried, "Kenny can*not* stay here, in this house. It just can't happen."

Mom smiled at me in that annoying way parents do sometimes. She walked over to the hallway linen closet and took out some sheets for the guest room bed. With a sinking heart I realized that it was actually true. The Beast was going to live with us for ten *looong*, awful days.

"Honey," Mom said. "Goodness, the way you sound, it almost makes me worry that you and Kenny don't get along."

I bit my lip. "Don't get along" is putting it mildly. We can't stand each other. But so far, Kenny and I have tried to keep our parents from realizing it. The thing is, our parents are best friends. The Beaumonts and the McIlhennys have lived next door to each other since before Kenny and I were born. My dad and Kenny's dad work at the same big company. My mom and Mrs. McIlhenny do tons of stuff together. Our two families have even taken vacations together! It's like something out of a book. Or like *Romeo and Juliet*, except backward. We have star-crossed parents, or something. (Romeo and Juliet are from a famous play by Shakespeare. My mom and I read it together. That's one thing you should know about me. Books are superbig in my life. I love to read more than practically anything. I can almost always think of things in books that are similar to things happening in real life.)

Now Kenny had come down with chicken pox. He had probably done it just to upset me. As my mom had explained, Kenny couldn't fly to Canada with chicken pox. At first, his dad was going to miss the trip so he could stay home and take care of Kenny. Then my mom had suggested that Kenny stay with us while his folks were gone. And the McIlhennys had accepted! Thanks a lot, Mom. Thank you for completely destroying the next ten days of my life.

As Mom bustled off, I slunk into my room. My room and the guest room were separated only by my bathroom. A horrible thought suddenly hit me: Kenny and I would be sharing a bathroom.

I moaned out loud and fell onto my bed. I buried my face in my pillow. How embarrassing! To share a bathroom with the Beast! A boy! I'm an only child, and I've never had boys around. Even my cousins are almost all girls. And of course, all my friends are girls.

Speaking of which, I was due to meet my friends at our neighborhood park soon to go in-line skating. The bad thing about living in Willow Hill is the fact that my worst enemy lives right next door. But it's almost worth it because four of my best friends live just blocks away in the same suburb. My *best* best friend lives farther away, in Wildwood Estates.

I felt a tiny bit better as I pulled my in-line skates out from under my bed and changed my socks. Soon I would be seeing Jasmine, Paula, Ella, Ariel, and Yukiko. They would be able to help me, I was sure of it. The six of us together can fix any problem, as long as we work on it together. That's because we have magic on our side. But I'll explain about that in a minute.

Chapter Two

Hellllp Meeee!

"*Look out!*" Paula yelled in back of me. I froze, putting my heel to the ground and rolling to a halt. Seconds later, Paula zoomed past me, her dark hair flying out from beneath her helmet. I had barely recovered from the swish of wind when Ariel skated past, rapidly gaining on Paula. I saw a fierce, triumphant grin on Ariel's face as she hunched down. There was a sharp curve on the path ahead of us, and I lost sight of Paula and Ariel as they careened around the corner.

"*Sheesh.* Those two," said Jasmine, rolling up next to me.

I nodded. "Everything is a race."

Oops. Have I jumped into the middle again? I have to quit doing that. Okay—let me clue you in.

The setting: Willow Green, the small park in the middle of our neighborhood.

The people: us—the six Disney Girls. That means me, Jasmine Prentiss, Paula Pinto, Ariel Ramos, Ella O'Connor, and Yukiko Hayashi. Ella and Yukiko were just catching up to me and Jasmine.

The background: it's a little tricky to explain. Basically, the six of us are all best friends. We're also three pairs of *best* best friends—three pairs of soul mates, kind of. Me and Jasmine, Paula and Ariel, and Ella and Yukiko. What Jasmine was commenting on was that Paula and Ariel are both very physical—and competitive. They love to run and jump and skate and swim and do everything as hard as they can. It almost always turns into a contest of some kind. They love trying to outdo each other. But their friendship is so special, they're actually pleased when the other one bests them at something. (Go figure.)

Confused yet? Wait—there's more. But I saw that Paula and Ariel had flopped down on the grass beneath some pine trees. The rest of us skated over to join them.

"Whew," said Ariel, blowing some of her bright red hair out of her eyes. "That last turn almost wiped me out." Her face looked damp with sweat. Even though it was only May, summer had already arrived in Orlando. It was in the low nineties, and we were steaming. I started to think about how we could all get rides over to Jasmine's house—and her swimming pool.

"Tuck down and lean to the left," Paula advised, still panting. She flapped her T shirt a couple of times to cool off.

I lay back on the sun-warmed grass. It was a beautiful day, I was with my best friends, everything seemed perfect. Until I remembered that it was T minus four hours until the Beast showed up at my door. I groaned out loud.

"What's wrong?" asked Ella, concerned. "Do you have a blister?"

"No," I said, "though I *will* have a painful irritation soon."

Jasmine giggled.

"What are you talking about?" Yukiko asked.

"Kenny," Jasmine answered for me. "He's arriving tonight."

Five sympathetic glances came my way. They knew the whole story, of course. They had even suffered at the Beast's hands before. But that's another story.

You may have noticed that I call Kenny "the Beast." I do that for a couple of reasons. Mostly, it's because he's beastly. But hey, what's new about that, you ask. He is a *boy*, right? But there's another reason Kenny's the Beast. It has to do with my being Belle, from *Beauty and the Beast*. I'm Belle, Kenny's the Beast—get it? Only, he's the Beast before he turned into the prince, if you know what I'm saying.

Are you wondering about the whole Disney Girl/*Beauty and the Beast* thing? (Maybe you aren't, if you've already read about us.) But maybe you are. I wish I could explain exactly what a Disney Girl is. All I can tell you is that my five best friends and I are Disney Girls. That means we have a magical connection to certain Disney princesses— and to each other. For example, I'm Belle. I mean, I *know* I'm African American, with dark brown eyes, tan skin, and dark, short, braided hair. Nevertheless, I just *am* Belle, and you'll have to take my word for it.

Jasmine is Princess Jasmine, from *Aladdin*. (When we first met, I didn't realize it right away. But once I saw past

Jasmine's blonde hair, green eyes, and freckles, it was totally obvious.) Paula is Pocahontas. After all, Paula is Native American, with dark hair, beautiful tan skin, and dark brown eyes. Ella is Cinderella, of course. She even has a stepmother and two stepsisters. Not to mention her pet mice! (Her stepmom and stepsisters aren't yucky, though.)

Who do you know who has red hair, blue eyes, swims like a fish, and has a bunch of sisters? Sound familiar? Does the name Ariel ring a bell? Ariel is Ariel, the Little Mermaid. You practically don't even have to be a Disney Girl to realize that. The last DG is Yukiko. The first time you look at her, you might not snap your fingers and say, "Snow White! Of course!" But if you talked to her for five minutes, you wouldn't believe that you didn't see it before. Her name even means "snow" in Japanese. (Yukiko is Japanese American.) And get this— she has six little brothers and one baby sister. The Seven Dwarfs!

Later on I'll tell you more about how we found each other, and how we realized that we were Disney Girls. Right now I had to tell my friends about the doom hanging over my head.

"I'll actually have to share a bathroom with the Beast!" I wailed.

"*Eww!*" said Ella, wrinkling her nose.

"No duh," I grumbled. "It's my worst nightmare come true. And there's nothing I can do about it."

"You could play mean tricks on him," suggested Ariel. "Like, put salt in his milk, or short-sheet his bed."

"Yeah," I said doubtfully.

"Or you could just wait and see how he is," suggested Paula. (Paula is almost always really reasonable.) "Maybe he'll be so sick, he'll leave you alone."

"I can always hope," I agreed.

"How sick is he going to be, anyway?" Ariel asked. "I mean, is he going to be barfing, or what?"

"No, no barfing," I said. "I think with chicken pox you just feel a little yucky, and then you itch all over. I had it so long ago I don't remember."

"How much school will he miss?" asked Ariel. Was that a gleam in her eye?

"A week," I said.

"Jeez! I would love to miss a week of school!" said Ariel. "Is the Beast still contagious?"

"Oh, gross," said Yukiko.

11

"Hey!" said Ariel. "One less week of school might be worth getting close to Kenny for. This could work out great."

Paula rolled her eyes. "Can I change the subject?"

"Please," I said.

"I'd like to announce that Jasmine and I have gotten our white belts," Paula said. "We're official tae kwon do students."

"Yay!" the rest of us cheered.

"Good for you," I said proudly.

Paula and Jasmine looked pleased. A little while ago, Paula had taken a week-long karate class at the Disney Institute, at Walt Disney World. She had loved it! Since then, she and Jasmine had signed up for tae kwon do (tye-kwan-doh) at a dojo in Willow Hill. (Tae kwon do is a kind of karate. A dojo is a place to study it—like a dance studio.) They were going once a week, on Tuesday afternoons. I didn't know this, but you start out with no belt at all. After a month you take a test, and the teacher either weeds you out or you get your white belt.

"Now what?" asked Ella.

"Now we work toward our yellow belt," said Paula.

"Cool," I said. Then I had an idea. "Hey! Maybe you

guys could quickly teach me enough karate to put the hurt on Kenny."

My friends laughed.

"Sorry," Jasmine said, grinning. "That's not what karate's about."

"Dang," I said. I would have to come up with something else.

Chapter Three

The Poxman Cometh

That night after dinner, I was in my room doing my homework when the doorbell rang. I groaned, then forced myself to my feet and clomped to the living room.

Kenny and his mom stood there, being greeted by my parents.

"Thank you so much, Michelle," Mrs. McIlhenny was saying.

"Oh, Delia, please, it's no problem," said Mom. "We're happy to do it."

My eyes widened at this blatant lie. Maybe *she* was happy to do it, but *we* sure weren't.

Kenny caught my eyes and grinned. It wasn't a nice grin. My stomach dropped. This was going to be an awful ten days.

"Woof!" Otto barked happily when he saw my dogs. Snuffles and Pokey bounded in from the kitchen, yipping hello. *Snarl,* I commanded them mentally. *Growl fiercely.* Instead, Snuffles, Pokey, and Otto bounced merrily around each other, sniffing and making friendly sounds. Who said animals are telepathic?

"I better run," said Mrs. McIlhenny. "Our flight leaves in two hours. You're quite sure this is okay?"

"Of course," said Mom, waving her hand. "No problem. I have your hotel number in Ontario. You guys just go off and have a good time."

"All right then," said Kenny's mom. She leaned over and kissed him. He looked embarrassed. "Bye, honey. I hope you don't feel too bad. If you need me, you just call, and we'll come right home, okay?"

"Yeah, sure," said Kenny.

"Thanks again, Michelle," said Kenny's mom, hugging my mom. "Someday we'll return the favor."

"Sure," said Mom. "Bye, now."

Mom, if you ever leave me with the McIlhennys for ten days, I will kill you, I threatened silently.

After the front door closed, Mom put her arm around Kenny's shoulder. "How do you feel, honey?" she asked.

Kenny looked up at her earnestly. "Okay, I guess," he said. "I just have a little bit of a sore throat."

The way he said it would make someone think he was really on the verge of a coma, but putting on a brave front.

"Poor thing," Mom said, while I tried not to gag. "Let's get you settled."

Kenny nodded sadly, and followed my mom to the guest room. When he passed me he let his lips curl up in a smirk. I felt my hands clench. I decided to go downstairs and watch TV.

"Sweetie?" Mom called. "Can you come help?"

I stopped in my tracks. Come help? Was she kidding? She was the one who had agreed to this.

"Isabelle?" called Mom.

My eyes wide in disbelief, I stomped through the dining room, down the hall, and to the door of the guest room. Mom was busily folding back the covers of the bed.

Kenny, wearing sweatpants and a T-shirt, was getting ready to clamber in. Otto was sitting nearby, panting and already drooling disgustingly. (Otto is a bloodhound. If you have never been up close and personal with a blood-hound, let me tell you: they are big. And they slobber. They have long, loose jowls that hang down, and actual *threads of slobber* dangle off them. I am not making this up. This was happening in my own house.)

"Yeah?" I asked.

"Honey, could you get one of the little TV tables from the closet?" Mom asked. "We can set one up here by the side of the bed."

Kenny got into bed and leaned back against the extra pillows, looking like every movement was causing him great pain.

"Uh-huh," I said, spinning on my heel. I got the TV table, and Mom popped it open near the head of the bed. She asked me to get a cold 7Up for Kenny. I gnashed my teeth, wondering if we had anything yucky I could put into his drink. After all, I am almost never allowed to drink soda, unless it's a party or something.

I brought in a can of 7Up and a cup with ice and plunked them down on the TV tray. Kenny smiled wanly at me, and my mom smiled at him and brushed his dark hair off his forehead. I began to feel nauseated. Then Otto lumbered up on the bed next to Kenny. Oh, no, I thought. That dog's going to drool on our bed.

I waited for Mom to shoo Otto off, but she didn't. Kenny rubbed Otto's big, floppy ears and put on a brave face. I wanted to smack him. Then, you won't believe this, I actually felt a teensy bit guilty. I mean, Kenny *was* sick. It wasn't his fault that he couldn't go to Canada with his parents. He probably already missed them. And even though it was his fault that he was obnoxious, still, I should probably cut him some slack. As long as he was truly sick.

I was thinking these forgiving thoughts when I realized my mom was wheeling in the little TV from my dad's home office. My mouth dropped open. I would have to be on my deathbed before my mom would bring the TV into my room! Didn't she always say that TV rots your brain? Didn't she always say that a sick person couldn't rest and watch TV at the same time? Didn't she always say that daytime TV was the curse of modern civilization?

And yet, here she was, my own mother, handing my worst enemy the remote control. I felt like my whole world was cracking apart. I stared first at her, then at Kenny. Mom didn't notice—she was still fussing over him, putting a box of tissues on the TV tray. But Kenny saw me. He gave me a fake sick grin, managing to look humble and totally slimy at the same time. I swallowed hard and decided to leave before I said something that Mom would make me regret.

In my room, I fell face first onto my bed, moaning pathetically into my pillow. Ten days was going to be a long, long time. Almost without realizing it, I found myself calling on magic:

> "All the magic powers that be,
> Hear me now, my special plea.
> It's Belle. The Beast is looking pale.
> If I kill him, will I go to jail?"

While I waited for magic's answer, a warm feeling came over me. The whole situation suddenly seemed ridiculous and funny at the same time. I rolled over on my back and giggled. I thought about what I had faced in my movie, and what I was facing now. Holding my sides, I laughed and laughed.

Chapter Four

Mr. Murchison

On Monday, Paula, Ariel, Ella, Yukiko, and I all rode the school bus to Orlando Elementary, as usual. Since Jasmine lives in Wildwood Estates, her mom usually drives her to school. I wish she could take the bus, too.

Anyway, she was waiting for us by the school gates.

I jumped off the bus and grabbed my backpack. "Oops!" I said. The zipper looked like it was starting to unravel. I tucked everything back in and slung it on my shoulders again.

"How's it going with the Beast?" Jasmine asked.

"Ugh," I said. "My mom is fussing over him like you wouldn't believe. It's disgusting."

"Doesn't she fuss over you when you're sick?" Ella asked.

"Well, yeah," I admitted. "Except she's never moved the TV into my room. And also, I'm hardly ever sick. And, of course, the fact that it's Kenny makes everything worse."

"I can understand that," Paula said. "Well, it's only ten days. It'll be over before you know it."

Sometimes Paula is a little *too* reasonable, if you know what I mean.

Yukiko leaned close. "Have you tried magic?" she asked in a low voice.

I nodded. "Uh-huh. I mean, I haven't asked for any help, really. It's more like I just kind of complained to magic."

The school bell rang. Ariel, Ella, and Yukiko headed off to third grade. Jasmine, Paula, and I went upstairs to Mr. Murchison's fourth-grade class. Actually, I should be in third grade. (I turned nine only a few weeks ago.) But I read at a much higher level than most kids my age, so I had skipped second grade, back at my old school.

I like Mr. Murchison. He tries to make learning interesting, and he doesn't just stick to our textbooks. He uses lots of different tools to teach us about things.

Today, after he took roll, he walked to the middle of the classroom. (That's another good thing about Mr. Murchison. He walks all around, as if he were one of us, instead of standing at the front of the room always being the Teacher.)

"You know, guys," he said. "I saw this neat exhibit at the museum over the weekend. It was all about genealogy. Do y'all know what genealogy is?"

Allison Mason raised her hand. "Like, your family tree?"

"Yes, pretty much," said Mr. Murchison. "Genealogy is the study of a person's, or a group's, lineage. Their history. Their ancestors. And sometimes, examining someone's genealogy can go a long way to explaining, discovering, and exploring who someone is, and why they are the way they are."

I sat happily in my seat, thinking, I love school.

"It gave me an idea about a project we could do ourselves," continued Mr. Murchison. "It would combine research, writing, and an oral report." He smiled. "My three favorite things. And yours, too, I'm sure."

I giggled.

"So!" he said, clapping his hands once. "Here it is: I

want each of you to research your own family tree. It could simply be asking your parents, grandparents, or other relatives about themselves and any ancestors they remember. It could be looking at written family documents, such as family bibles, family trees, old letters, stuff like that. Maybe there are photographs. Maybe there are paintings. Explore, and ask your parents for help.

"Then, I want each of you to choose your favorite relative or ancestor. It can be someone still living, but I think it might be more interesting if it were someone from further back. It's up to you. Then, after you've researched your person, we'll take turns presenting oral reports. You can pretend to be your ancestor, wearing a costume if necessary, and try to give us a good and realistic picture of what your life was like."

"Cool," I breathed. I glanced over at Paula, and her dark eyes were shining. Jasmine turned around and gave me a thumbs-up. She thought it was a great assignment, too.

"These reports will be due next Monday," Mr. Murchison finished.

I raised my hand. "Um, Kenny McIlhenny's parents are out of town. How can he research his ancestors?" To myself I thought, he could always try the local animal shelter.

"Good point," said Mr. Murchison. "Let's see. He has access to a computer, right? Tell you what. Kenny's assignment will be a two-page paper on the history of the city of Orlando. He can easily research that on the Internet. Maybe your parents can help him a little." (My mom had sent Mr. Murchison a note explaining about Kenny.)

"Okay," I said. "I'll tell him."

My assignment was going to be much more fun than the Beast's.

Chapter Five

Chicken Pox Is Too Good for Him

Since you know that I'm Belle, you've probably figured out that my dad is an inventor. (He really is.) My mom works, too—she owns Beaumont's, which is a fancy food store. She sells all sorts of weird and interesting and fabulous foods that she imports from all over. A lot of times, instead of getting off the school bus at home, the driver lets me off at Beaumont's, and I hang out there. I don't like going home to an empty house, though I know lots of kids have to.

All this week, though, Mom was going to be home, taking care of the Beast. I let myself in the front door. The whole house seemed quiet.

"Hello?" I called.

"In here, honey," said Mom.

I sighed, dumped my backpack, and headed for the guest room. Inside I saw that Kenny was putting on a good show. When I looked carefully, though, he did look like he felt pretty yucky. He lay back against the pillows. The TV was off. Mom was taking his temperature.

"Hmm, almost a hundred and one," she murmured. "No wonder you feel lousy. I'll give you some medicine."

I was turning to go get myself a snack, since my own mother was obviously too busy with Kenny to care if I fainted from hunger or not, when Mom finally seemed to realize I was there.

"Hi, sweetie," she said, pouring Kenny a glass of juice. "How was school?"

"Fine," I said.

"Teacher's pet," Kenny muttered.

I narrowed my eyes at him. Mom pretended she hadn't heard him. "Here, chew these up," she said, handing him two tablets.

"Yuck," Kenny complained.

Can you believe that he complained to my mother, who was taking such good care of him? I wanted to give him a knuckle sandwich. I felt my jaw get firm, then I dropped his schoolbooks on the bed. I set a piece of paper on top of them. "Here are all your homework assignments," I said.

Kenny's brown eyes stared at me. He fell back against the pillows. "What?" he croaked.

I gave him a sickly sweet smile, the kind that parents never seem to see through. "I knew you wouldn't want to fall behind," I said kindly.

Kenny's nostrils flared.

"That was very thoughtful of you, honey," said my mom.

See?

Kenny snorted. I was about to tell him about our research assignment, but my mom said, "Isabelle, can you take poor Otto for a walk? I'm afraid he really needs some exercise."

"What?" I said.

Kenny's look of outrage changed to a sneaky smirk. When Otto heard his name, he raised his head and thumped his tail. His big, sad eyes looked hopefully at me. I turned and stalked out of the room, grabbing Otto's leash.

As soon as the bloodhound heard his leash jingle, he bounded off the bed and raced after me, brushing his slobbery lips against my leg in his hurry to get to the front door.

"*Eww!*" I cried. "*Eww! Eww!*" I grabbed a paper towel and wiped off my leg. Then I snapped Otto's leash on and we headed out.

If you have never taken a bloodhound for a walk, let me tell you: it is not the most fun you could ever imagine having. For one thing, they are great big dogs, so it feels like your arm is about to be pulled out of its socket. For another thing, they are scent dogs, tracking dogs. That means they get all excited about every tiny little stupid thing they smell, which is like five kajillion things in one city block. Then they have to race after it and track it down, which means your arm gets more pulled out of its socket. And I haven't even mentioned the whole outdoor-slobber factor, which gets really bad when they're smelling something and racing after it. Get the picture?

By the time I got home, I had leaves in my hair, grass stains on my knees (and I was wearing a skirt), and scratches on my arms from the Albionis's hedge when Otto was chasing a poor, defenseless squirrel who must have smelled especially good.

I looked like heck. I wanted to lie down on the couch with a wet rag draped over my forehead.

Inside, Otto eagerly slurped up his bowl of water. My mom was in the kitchen, starting to get dinner. She gave me a sympathetic smile.

"Poor baby," she said softly. "Otto is a handful, isn't he?"

I nodded and parked myself in a kitchen chair. I was hot and dirty and scratched all over. Mom held out a cold, frosty can of 7Up. My eyes widened. What a treat! Would it ever taste fabulous! I reached for the can, so happy that Mom was taking pity on me. But her next words were like cold water splashed in my face.

"Can you take this to Kenny, please?" she said.

My face fell in disappointment. I took the can silently and headed for Kenny's room.

In his room, he took one look at me and started laughing. Laughing made him cough, so he sat up and hacked for a while. I set the can on his bedside table and folded my arms. I was *soooo* angry. I was angry at him, at Otto, at my mom, and at the whole unfair situation. Before I knew it, words just popped out of my mouth.

"By the way, Kenny," I said. "I forgot to tell you about

29

our research assignment. The rest of us have to research our family, but you can't, so you have to do a paper on the history of Orlando. You can use our computer if you want."

Kenny stopped laughing. "A research paper? But I'm sick."

"You're not too sick to be a fink to me," I pointed out. "So I guess you can do your paper. It's due next Monday."

Kenny's face took on a sullen frown. I already felt a little better.

"How long is the paper, teacher's pet?" he asked.

There was that name again. My fists clenched. "Ten pages," I heard myself say. We were both surprised.

"Ten pages!" Kenny exclaimed. "No way! We're only in fourth grade. There's no way that Murch would give us that."

I shrugged. "So don't do it," I said. "I don't care. But that's the assignment." To tell you the truth, I was amazed at myself. I mean, even though Kenny is always ticking me off, it doesn't come naturally to me to be mean to someone, or to lie. It was like an evil fairy was sitting on my shoulder, making me say these things. The thing that really worried me was that I was enjoying it.

"Ten pages," Kenny repeated in shock. "I don't believe it. Ten pages handwritten?"

"Typed." Ooh, I was bad.

The Beast flopped back against his pillows. His face looked flushed. He gave a little cough.

"Jeez, ten pages," he said weakly. "That'll take me forever. All about Orlando? Jeez."

"Better get started," I advised, and left the room. That's me: the Wicked Witch of the South.

Chapter Six

In Search of an Ancestor

The amazing thing about meanness is how easy it is to continue, once you've started. It had been a big deal to give the Beast the much-too-long assignment, but it was easy to keep it up as the week went on. Kenny made it a snap: every time I felt a twinge of guilt and decided to tell him the truth, he would be icky to me, and my heart would turn to an icy stone again, just like Princess Bitterberry in that book *The Elf Wars*.

Take Wednesday. At school during library time I had found a few books about where my parents are from. I thought it would help me get a feel for my ancestors. My mom's family is from Jamaica, which is an island in the West Indies, and my dad's family is from Louisiana. I mean, both my parents' families were originally from Africa, of course. But that was a pretty long time ago.

Anyway, I had taken out a book on Jamaica and a book on the history of Louisiana. They were really interesting, and I decided that when I got home, I would look on the Internet for more info. But guess who greeted me when I raced through my front door after school? The Beast, using the computer.

He was hunched over the keyboard, frowning. Piles of messy papers surrounded him. His hair was all wild, as if he had been pulling it. He was wearing his chicken pox outfit: a T-shirt and sweatpants.

"Hi, sweetie," said my mom. She set a cup of iced tea at Kenny's elbow. (I'm never allowed to have food or drinks around the computer.) "Guess what? Kenny's fever is all gone." She smiled. "He should be breaking out in spots any moment now." Mom gave me a quick kiss and headed back to the kitchen. No "How are you?" No "Have a good day?" Nope. Just iced tea for Kenny.

"I need the computer," I told him.

"Tough," Kenny said absently. "Did you know that cowboys used to wrestle alligators on Magnolia Avenue a hundred years ago?" He peered at the computer screen. I saw that he was looking at a web site for Orlando. He was going to have a hard time coming up with ten pages of Orlando's history.

There it was again. The sudden urge to tell him the truth, and let him off the hook. You know, it's harder to get in touch with magic when you're spending energy being mean to someone. Usually all of us Disney Girls can feel magic surrounding us, giving us all sorts of possibilities. The last few days, magic had felt kind of dull and dim. I had to make a choice: did I want to be a source of good in the world, or a source of bad feelings?

I opened my mouth. "Ken—"

"By the way," Kenny interrupted. "Your Walkman needs new batteries. I was listening to it today, and I ran them down. It's a dinky little machine, anyway."

If I were a cat, my ears would have gone back, flat against my head. My mouth snapped shut. I said, "Quit hogging the computer. The rest of us have assignments, too." I left the Beast to his horrible, impossible report.

After dinner, I was helping my parents clean up the kitchen. Dad was rinsing the dishes, and I was loading them into the dishwasher. I seized the chance to quiz them about our ancestors.

"Okay, now," I said. "Do we have anyone famous? Any celebrities?"

"I don't think so," my mom said, wiping down a counter. "We're not related to Denzel Washington or Maya Angelou, if that's what you're asking."

Drat. "Dad, how about a famous inventor, like George Washington Carver?"

"Not that I know of, honey," said Dad, handing me the last plate. "Just me." He dried his hands and headed downstairs to his basement workshop, where he tinkers with his latest projects.

"Dancers, like Judith Jamison?" I asked Mom. "War heroes, like Crispus Attucks? Civil rights activists, like Rosa Parks?"

Mom frowned in thought. "No, I'm afraid not." Her face brightened. "Your grandfather had one of the biggest hardware stores in Kingston, Jamaica."

That wasn't what I was looking for.

"How about Dad's family? Did any of his ancestors join

the Underground Railroad to escape slavery in Louisiana?" I asked hopefully.

"I don't think so," Mom said. "I'm not sure his people were ever slaves. I think they came over as freemen. You'll have to ask him."

"How could they not be slaves?" I argued. "I mean, blacks in Louisiana before the Civil War?"

"It's a good research project, all right," Mom said with a smile. She handed me a sponge. "Could you please help me wipe down the cupboard doors? Otto has been flinging slobber in here again."

That was my life. Even though I'm a Disney princess, even though I'm blessed with the gift of magic, even though I have five of the best friends anyone could ever possibly have—still, here I was: no famous relatives—just dog slobber. Lots of dog slobber. I looked up in time to see Kenny heading for the bathroom. He gave me a smirk. I bet he had never wiped up Otto's slobber in his life. I wanted to throw the sponge at his head.

I've got this all wrong, I thought as I began the gross task. I'm not Belle. I should be Cinderella.

Chapter Seven

Come Here, Spot

"Oh, good morning, Kenny," Mom said brightly at breakfast on Thursday. "You look like you feel better. Are you up to joining us?"

"Yes, thanks," said Kenny, sliding into a seat across from me. I looked at him. He did seem as if he *felt* better. That didn't mean he *looked* better. In fact, he looked much worse. He was covered with small pink spots, as if someone had been playing connect-the-dots with his face.

Kenny smiled at me innocently from across the table.

He held up one arm and scratched it. Now, if it were Jasmine or any of the other DGs covered with spots, I would have felt sorry for her. I wouldn't have thought it was gross. I would have been happy to do all I could to make her feel better.

Kenny was a different story. It seemed as if he was enjoying his spots.

"I look like I have the plague," he announced cheerfully, reaching for the milk.

"Or leprosy," I offered.

"*Isabelle*," Mom said.

Kenny examined his arm. "Hey! You're right! It does kind of look like leprosy." He took a big spoonful of cereal. "Cool."

Okay now: I ask you. What kind of a person thinks that would be cool? A beastly kind of person, that's who. I put my head down and shoveled in my breakfast. I couldn't wait to get to school.

"So is he still contagious?" Ariel asked at lunchtime.

The six of us Disney Girls always sit at the third table down from the windows in the cafeteria. I'd been so rattled this morning, I had just grabbed the first things I saw in the fridge. Luck had been with me: lunch was a small wedge of Brie cheese, some water crackers, a chunk of Italian sausage, and some little French cornichons. (Those are tiny pickles.) I love all of those things.

"Yes," I answered, cutting myself a slice of cheese and balancing it on a cracker. "I think he'll be contagious for another forty-eight hours or so."

Ariel's blue eyes gleamed. "Can I come over after school today?"

"Sure," I said. "But don't you—oh. Oh, no! Ariel—you aren't thinking—"

Ariel took a bite of her school lunch: Beefaroni cheese. Now you know why I try to bring mine from home. "Uh-huh," she said, after she had swallowed. "If he's contagious, I have a shot at missing a whole week of school."

Paula groaned. "Oh, Ariel. That is so lame."

"Ariel, you would have to get pretty close to Kenny," Jasmine pointed out. "Like, you might have to touch him. Or let him sneeze on you."

We all made yucky faces at this thought.

"I can handle a minute of extreme ew-yosity for a whole week of hanging around, watching TV," said Ariel.

I sighed to myself. I recognized that determined look

she had. It usually meant we were all going to be in trouble soon.

"Not to change the subject, but can I have a little of your Brie?" asked Jasmine. That's one of the many things that my best best friend and I have in common: we both love to try new foods. The other DGs pretty much stick with the basics, although Paula's a vegetarian.

"Sure," I said, cutting her a piece. "Are those pierogis you have?"

"Take some," Jasmine offered, pushing over her lunch.

"How are your reports going?" Paula asked.

"Are these your ancestor reports?" Ella asked. She finished her sandwich and started on her apple. I've noticed that Ella always eats one thing at a time, and finishes it before she starts the next thing. It's always sandwich, fruit, dessert. Never half a sandwich, part of her fruit, more sandwich, more fruit, dessert. Never dessert first. I don't know why I'm telling you this. I just noticed it, is all.

"Uh-huh," said Jasmine. She sighed. "I think this report is going to bring my grade *waaay* down."

"Why?" Yukiko asked.

"I hate to admit it," said Jasmine, "but all my ancestors

40

stink. The only possibilities I've been able to come up with are from either my mom's family or my dad's family."

"No duh," said Ariel impatiently.

"On my mom's side," Jasmine continued, "her family mostly had the largest plantation in northern Georgia."

That didn't sound too bad. "What did they grow?" I asked.

Jasmine grimaced. "Tobacco."

We all gasped.

"Whoa," said Paula. "I see what you mean."

"Yeah. So on my mom's side, we were growing cancer plants with slaves," said Jasmine. "There's no way I'm admitting that in class. And on my dad's side, the only person he could come up with was old Tippy Prentiss."

"Was he royalty or something?" Yukiko asked. (Jasmine's dad is from England.)

"Oh, I don't know," said Jasmine. "Probably he was a minor baronet. But the main thing Tippy was famous for was riding his father's best hunting horse up the main staircase during a weekend house party."

"Hmm," I said. That didn't sound too promising.

"Keep looking," said Ella encouragingly. "I'm sure you've got better people than that."

"I'm having trouble, too," said Paula. "You'd think with being Native American and all, I'd have fabulous ancestors growing on trees. But *nooo*. My research has turned up Great-uncle Happy, who was a very successful plumber in Okeechobee, or my aunt Melissa, who makes quilts. I mean, her quilts are totally awesome. But still."

"No legendary warriors?" I asked.

"No cool, mystical medicine women?" suggested Ella.

"Nope." Paula looked frustrated. "I guess I'll have to keep digging."

"Hey, how's Kenny doing on his Orlando history?" asked Jasmine, turning to me.

I took a sip of juice, hoping my face wasn't turning red. I hadn't told my friends about the awful trick I was playing on Kenny. I guess it's because I knew it was pretty rotten. I wanted to confess it to someone—but right now I couldn't.

"I think he's doing okay," I said, trying to sound casual. "He's been totally hogging the computer."

"I can't wait to see what he looks like," said Ariel with a grin. "Chicken pox, here I come!"

Chapter Eight

Gimme Some Skin

When Ariel and I got home on Thursday afternoon, we found: Mom in the kitchen, trying a new olive-salad recipe for Beaumont's; Snuffles, Pokey, and Otto all asleep together in a snoring, furry pile on the dog bed in the family room; and Kenny, hunched tensely over a pile of messy index cards in front of the computer.

"Hey, Spot Boy," Ariel said, dropping her book bag on the sofa. I dropped mine next to hers, and the zipper split open. My books and notebooks slid to the floor.

I sighed and picked them all up.

Kenny looked around and pretended to be frightened. "Ariel! Your hair's on fire! Quick, somebody, put it out!"

Ariel rolled her eyes and flung her bright red hair over her shoulder. "Oh, please," she yawned. "I've been hearing that since I was two years old. Try to do better next time, okay?" She reached out to pat him on the shoulder, but he pulled away.

"I don't want your cooties," he said, getting up and heading for the kitchen.

"Yeah, Ariel," I said. "He already looks like the Creature from the Pox Lagoon. Why make it worse?"

Ariel and I snickered at each other, then followed the Beast into the kitchen for a snack.

You know, chicken pox is spread by either direct contact (that means touching someone's actual germs, like on their hand) or through the respiratory system (which means breathing someone's germs up your nose—gross!). So Ariel kept trying to get as close to Kenny as she could. He shot her weird looks and avoided her. I wondered if my mom knew what Ariel was up to, but she must have figured Ariel had already had CP.

"How was school today, girls?" my mom asked. She

held out a wooden spoon covered with olive salad. "Taste." Behind my mom's back, Kenny made a face. Probably his idea of good food was, like, a bologna sandwich on white bread with mayo.

I took a bite. "Hmm. It's good. But maybe a little more salt and a touch more garlic."

Mom laughed. "You always want more salt. But I'll try it."

"Yes, girls, how *was* school today?" Kenny mimicked.

I frowned at him. "Fine. How was daytime TV? Did Marcia leave Rick after she found out that KC had kidnapped Dawn so Philip wouldn't discover who the father of Janet's baby was?"

"And did you learn about a detergent that would make those whites whiter?" Ariel asked, pointing a carrot stick at him.

Kenny's eyes narrowed. I swear, he is so easy to tease, it's almost not even fun.

"Now, girls," said Mom. "Kenny was actually working very hard on his research paper most of the day."

I enjoyed seeing Kenny's face turn a sickly shade of green when he thought about his report. It was a very interesting effect, combined with the red poxes.

"Isn't Orlando a fascinating place?" I asked innocently.

"Yes, but ten pages does seem like an awful lot, doesn't
it?" said Mom.

"Ten pages!" Ariel said, looking confused. "Ow!"

I had kicked her under the table. She gave me a look
that said "Are you insane?"

"Oh, girls," said my mom. "Could you two please take
Otto for a walk? He went out in the backyard earlier with
Snuff and Poke, but he really needs more exercise than
those two."

There it was again. My ears went back like a cat's. Across
the table, Kenny grinned his beastly grin. I pictured what
he would look like covered with olive salad, and decided it
would be a waste of perfectly good olive salad.

"But Mom," I said, "Ariel came over to—"

"No, it's okay," Ariel said. "It'll be fun."

I stared at her. She didn't know what she was getting
into.

Ariel smiled at me. "You'll see."

"This is incredible!" I shouted to be heard above the
wind. I squinted my eyes as I hunkered down for more

control. Next to me, pedaling my bike as fast as she could, Ariel struggled to keep up with us.

We were in Willow Green. Otto was getting more exercise than he had ever gotten in his life. And I was having a blast! Ariel's brilliant idea had been for me to wear my in-line skates while I "walked" Otto. Otto is so big and strong, he could run and pull me on my skates at the same time. Now my hair was blowing straight back beneath my helmet, Otto was galloping with his ears streaming behind him and his tongue hanging out, and Ariel was pedaling hard.

"Go, Otto, go!" I yelled, streaking past other bikers, joggers, and kids playing. We were going so fast that Otto didn't have time to be distracted by scents. He really seemed to be enjoying it as much as I was. Who knew that "walking" a bloodhound could be so much fun?

Old sour-face Kenny was waiting for us by the front door when we arrived home, sweaty and happy.

"You didn't wear my dog out, did you?" he accused, grabbing Otto's leash. Otto bounded happily up the front steps and licked Kenny's face. I hoped Otto had already had chicken pox.

"Chill," I told Kenny. "He had a great time. You're just

mad because you've never thought of doing it yourself." I sat down on the steps and unbuckled my skates.

"He's a champion purebred bloodhound," Kenny snapped. "He's not supposed to be pulling girls on skates."

"Yeah, yeah, yeah," I said tiredly, waving my hand at him. I looked up to say more, but I noticed that Kenny's poxes were now dotted with pale pink blobs of calamine lotion. I smiled. "Itchy, are we?"

"Oh, can it," Kenny muttered.

Just then, my mom came out on the porch. "Here, sweetie," she told Kenny. "Time for more medicine." She gave him some pills that stop reactions like itching and sneezing. No wonder Kenny looked so tired and grumpy. I hate the way that medicine makes me feel. On top of everything, he'd been working on his TEN-page paper all day. Suddenly I felt really guilty. It was almost like I could feel my magic growing dim around me.

"Gosh!" Ariel said brightly. "Look at the time! I have to run!" She stood up, and before any of us knew what was happening, she grabbed Kenny and gave him a huge bear hug! It was her last shot at getting some of Kenny's germs. "Hope you feel better, Spot Boy," she said as she pranced down my front walk. "Bye, Isabelle!" Kenny looked like he wanted to bathe in disinfectant.

"Bye," I said, trying not to burst out laughing. That Ariel! She's too much.

Chapter Nine

Magic, Call Home

I had pored over all the family records I could come up with. I had visited some of the Jamaica web sites, trying to find out more about my mom's family. I had checked out a bunch of Louisiana stuff on the Internet and at the library. I was finding that both sides of my family were heavily into hardware stores.

Mom had mentioned that my grandfather had owned one of the largest hardware stores in Kingston, Jamaica. But she hadn't told me that my dad's family had also owned several different hardware stores all across

Louisiana. I mean, number one, what was the deal with all this hardware? And number two, why couldn't my family have had a slightly more interesting business?

"Dad, how could you be from Louisiana and not have any great jazz musicians in the family?" I complained on Saturday night. I had been working on my report all day, and I hadn't gotten anywhere. To tell you the truth, it was kind of freaking me out. I'm usually an A student. Reports are no big deal to me. I love doing research. I love writing. Yet here it was, Saturday night, and I had nothing. I wondered if it was because magic had sort of deserted me as soon as I had lied to Kenny. Of course, magic couldn't write my report for me. But when I feel really in touch with my magic, it's like the air itself is alive and humming with possibility. I feel extra creative, extra open to ideas, and more able to produce something.

Right now I felt like a lump of clay.

"Sorry, honey," Dad said, taking off his glasses and cleaning them. "We Beaumonts don't have a musical bone in our bodies. But by gum, I know a pipe wrench when I see it!"

The phone rang, and I raced to answer it.

"Hey," said Jasmine.

51

"Hi!" I said gratefully. "Oh, Jasmine, I am in so much trouble! I haven't even started my report!"

"You're not the only one," Jasmine said, sounding glum. "Get this—Mother has suggested Shugie Bingham, her aunt, as a good topic. Shugie is famous in Charlottesville for being the most popular debutante of the 1960 fall season. Shugie had seven marriage proposals before Christmas." Jasmine sighed.

"Whoa," I said sympathetically. "Now, if she had only married a Beaumont of Beaumont's Hardware, we would be even."

We laughed a little together.

"How's the Beast?" asked Jasmine.

"Spotty, but they're already not so itchy. He'll be fine by school on Monday," I said.

"Has he found two pages of stuff on Orlando?" Jasmine asked.

I was glad my *best* best friend couldn't see my face. "Yeah, I think so," I mumbled. Actually, it had been a little painful, listening to Kenny's anguished moans coming from the family room, where he was working. I had peeked in once, and saw the Beast huddled over the computer table, furiously copying down notes. Index cards were strewn everywhere; the wastepaper basket was full. He was having a really bad time.

"Um, I feel a little cut off from magic lately," I said, trying to sound unconcerned. "Do you think we could do a DG conference call?"

"Yeah, great idea!" said Jasmine. "I'll set it up and call you back." Jasmine's dad is a stockbroker, and he has an office at home. Jasmine can make huge conference calls from his office phone, when all six of us can talk at the same time.

A few minutes later, Jasmine called me back.

"Can everyone hear me?" she asked.

"Yep," I said.

"Loud and clear," said Paula.

"I'm here," said Ella.

"Me, too," Ariel said. "Make this fast—I'm about to watch *Ocean Girl* on TV." *Ocean Girl* is Ariel's favorite show.

"Oh, I love that show!" Yukiko said. "What channel does it come on?"

"Eleven," Ariel answered.

"Excuse me, guys," I said. "Could we just do a magic wish real quick?"

"Oh, sure," said Yukiko. "Sorry."

Holding the phone to my ear, I closed my eyes and concentrated. I took several deep breaths and tried to relax and let negative energy flow out and positive energy flow in. The image of Kenny's pink-spotted face floated before me. It was so irritating!

Anyway. I let another deep breath out and chanted with the others:

> "All the magic powers that be,
> Hear us now, our special plea.
> You know Belle's magic can't be found,
> Please help her know we're still around."

As soon as my friends and I finished this wish, I started to feel a little better. Just knowing that they cared and wanted to help made everything seem less overwhelming.

"Thanks, you guys," I said. "Now I can go try to find a good ancestor again."

"No prob," said Paula and the others agreed.

We chatted for a few minutes longer. You know what? There's nothing better than good friends. And I had the best friends in the world! After I hung up the phone, I went back to my room and sat at my desk. Resting my chin in my hands, I thought about my ancestors. Thousands of years of people having children had ended up with me as the end product. And who was I? I was a Disney princess. I was a great reader. I was someone who had not told my five best friends that I had pulled a really mean trick on Kenny McIlhenny.

Sighing, I leafed through Mom's old family bible again. Her family had been writing notes about their history for more than a hundred years. As I glanced down the list, a name caught my eye. "Halese St. Martin." Who was this?

"Hmm, Halese St. Martin," my mom murmured, when I asked her about it. "That name rings a bell. Let me look in this old file . . ."

An hour later it was past my bedtime, but I had found my ancestor! Halese St. Martin was the first black schoolteacher at the Ursuline Catholic school in Kingston, way back in 1884. She was my great-great-great-grandmother.

"This is perfect!" I crowed. "I can pretend I'm a schoolteacher, too! I wonder what she looked like."

My mom frowned in thought. Forty minutes later it was way past my bedtime. Mom and I were sitting in our attic, taking everything out of an ancient trunk that I hadn't even known we had. We had found a picture of Halese! She looked very solemn and formal. Her hair was pulled back tightly. She didn't look like any of my relatives. But she looked interesting and intelligent and different.

"Wait a minute," said Mom, rustling through some tissue in the trunk. "What's this?" She held up an old, old blouse, made out of rough cotton. It was stitched by hand very carefully. A tingle of magic went down my spine. It was the first magic I'd felt in days.

"Oh, Mom," I whispered shakily. "This is Halese's blouse. From the photo. Look!"

I held it next to the photo. Sure enough. It was the exact same blouse my ancestor had worn in the picture—probably the only photograph that had been taken of her in her whole life. And I was holding it. Right then I knew my report would be truly special.

Chapter Ten

The Gig Is Up

"Hey, way to go!" Alan Hill said, slapping Kenny a high five.

Kenny grinned and bounded onto the school bus. "Pretty gross, huh?"

"You look truly awesome, dude," Eric Morgenstein cackled.

I rolled my eyes and sat down next to Yukiko. "Of course, his lame friends would find chicken pox marks cool," I complained.

"Boys just cannot be figured out sometimes," Yukiko agreed.

Since I like school, I never dread Monday mornings. This morning, though, I was especially looking forward to class. I had worked on my report all day Sunday, and I was so proud of what I had gotten done. The best thing was having my ancestor's blouse and photograph. It really made it all come together.

At school Jasmine was waiting for us, as usual.

"Are you ready?" I asked her. I hitched up my backpack and pinched the zipper closed with my fingers.

"Yep," she said, her eyes crinkling at the edges.

"Me, too," said Paula. "I'm happy with what I came up with."

"I wish I could hear these reports," said Ella. "Fourth grade is so much better than third grade."

"Maybe you should do your reports for us at the next sleepover," suggested Ariel.

"I'll ask Mom if I can have it at my house next week, on Saturday," Yukiko offered.

"Yeah!" said Jasmine. "And we can go shopping the next day and get Isabelle a new backpack. Nature Girl has some cute ones."

I beamed. The whole week was going to be fabulous.

In class, I suddenly realized that I had a black cloud hanging over my head. It was my lying to Kenny. I looked over at him as Mr. Murchison called roll. The Beast was goofing around quietly with his friends. But anyone who knew him well (unfortunately, I do) would see that there were lines of tension on his face. I didn't even know if he had finished his ridiculously long report or not. I didn't see how he could have. I swallowed hard and looked down at my desk. I knew I had to change this situation.

"And that's the story," I finished up. I felt deeply embarrassed, and to cover it, I pulled my container of herb tea closer and took a sip. My five best friends sat around our lunch table silently.

I hadn't been brave enough to confess to the Beast right away. I knew I had to come clean to my friends first. I wondered what they were thinking.

"Wow," said Ariel. "That's just about the most awful thing I've ever seen you do." She grinned. "Way to go!"

"Ariel," Paula said. She turned to me. "I can see why you did it—but I can also see why you feel bad about it. What are you going to do now?"

"I have to tell Kenny before we give our reports, this afternoon," I said. "But I really hate the idea."

"You mean all week, while he's been sick, Kenny's been panicking, thinking he has to write a ten-page report about Orlando?" said Ella.

"Yeah, that's what I said," I mumbled.

Ella snickered, and covered her mouth with her hand. Then Yukiko's mouth twitched, and she tried to hide her laughter. Ariel started laughing outright, and even Jasmine and Paula smiled.

"Oh, thank you," I said irritably. "Thank you for encouraging me to be a force of evil."

"You're not evil," Jasmine said, putting her arm around my shoulders. "You're just—Belle. And he's the Beast. These things are going to happen."

"I hope Kenny sees it that way," I said.

The Beast was hanging with his beastly pals out on the basketball court in the school yard. The DGs wished me luck, and watched as I set off toward Kenny. My shoulders were straight, my head held high, my eyes looked forward. I was as ready as I would ever be. (Which was not very, if you want to know the truth.)

Kenny had his back to me as I approached. I pictured him looking angry, then relieved, then angry again. I was so glad that this would all be over soon, and I could feel good about myself again.

Kenny's voice wafted back to me, carried on a breeze.

"Yeah, what can I say? Her folks are decent, but she's a royal pain. I mean, I look awful because I have chicken pox. But what's her excuse?"

Alan and Eric snickered, and I froze in my tracks. I couldn't believe that Kenny would be so casually mean about me to his friends. Especially after my mom had been taking such good care of him for a week! Even though the Beast and I are best enemies, still, my feelings were really hurt.

Then I got mad. I had been coming over here to confess to him, and to apologize, and here he was, talking bad about me behind my back! What a jerk! My heart hardened once more, and I turned on my heel to head back to my friends.

In my opinion, the Beast deserved everything I dished out. I should have made it a *twenty*-page report!

Chapter Eleven

My Ancestor

"Okay, now for the moment we've all been waiting for," said Mr. Murchison later that afternoon. "I hope everyone's ready to give a completely fascinating account of their favorite or most interesting relative. Now, who should go first?"

I shot my hand up, and so did about eight other kids. Kenny tried to make himself small in his desk chair. Of course, this sent a signal to Mr. Murchison that he should be called on.

"Kenny?" asked Mr. Murchison. "How about we start

with you? Glad to have you back, by the way. It looks like your beauty rest didn't quite have an effect, but that's okay."

I couldn't help chuckling. I love Mr. Murchison.

With a sickly smile, Kenny gathered a sheaf of papers and walked to the front of the room. "Um, I did the history of Orlando," he began unenthusiastically. "But I—I didn't quite finish it."

"But Kenny, you had a whole week," Mr. Murchison pointed out.

"I know," Kenny muttered. "But it was hard coming up with ten whole pages of stuff. I managed to get only seven."

I felt my face begin to burn.

"Ten? There must be some misunderstanding," said Mr. Murchison. "Each report was supposed to be only two pages."

Kenny's brown eyes went wide. "What?"

Mr. Murchison motioned Kenny over. The two of them huddled for a few moments, and Kenny handed in his seven pages of Orlando history. I waited for Mr. Murchison to call me up to explain exactly how Kenny had gotten the wrong assignment.

The weird thing was, he never did. Kenny sat down at his desk again, after shooting me a look that should have melted me on the spot. Then Mr. Murchison called on Allison Mason. She did her report on a cousin of hers who was in NASA. It was really interesting.

Jasmine's ancestor was hysterical. She had chosen the one black sheep of her mother's family: Baxter Holladay, who had been a rum runner during prohibition! That meant he had illegally sold whiskey and other alcohol when it was against the law, back in the 1930s! I bet Jasmine's mom must have been so embarrassed that Jasmine picked him.

Paula had decided to go with her aunt Melissa, who makes beautiful quilts. Dressed in normal clothes, Paula explained how each of her quilts told a story or myth about the history of the Seminole tribe. By using a traditional craft in a modern way, her aunt was able to combine old and new, and to express her creativity in a time-honored, traditionally female way. And her quilts *were* beautiful. The colors were gorgeous, and they were very detailed and intricate. Paula had chosen a terrific relative.

After Lani Watkins, Henry Booth, and Fernanda

Peña had gone, it was my turn. I was all ready. In the girls' bathroom, I had changed into Halese's blouse. I had pulled my hair back tightly, the way she had. When Mr. Murchison called on me, I walked slowly and steadily to the front of the room, trying to imagine that I really was Halese St. Martin, and I was back in Jamaica in the 1880s. I knew that I had to prove myself to everyone.

At first I was aware of Jasmine and Paula watching me and sending me good vibes, and I knew that Kenny's dark eyes were boring angry holes into me. Soon I forgot about all of them as I lost myself in Halese's story. I knew only a few details, but I had embroidered on these to make up a likely life story. I described how proud I was to be a teacher, and how important it was that blacks be given the same jobs and were treated the same as whites.

When my report was over, it was quiet in the classroom. I had ended by clasping my hands in my lap, and turning my head exactly the way Halese had in the photo. I had wanted to look as much like her as possible.

Jasmine was the first to start clapping, followed by Paula, and slowly, the rest of the class. I was so proud. I didn't look at Kenny. But in my heart, I doubted that

Halese would have played such a mean trick on anyone—no matter how much they hurt her feelings.

I thought more about Halese as I changed back into my own T-shirt. I folded my ancestor's blouse carefully and tucked it on top of everything in my backpack. Halese had struggled to rise above her poor circumstances. She had worked hard and made something positive of herself—a schoolteacher. My cheeks felt hot when I walked back into the classroom and saw the Beast's stiff face. I felt as if I had let Halese down. I would have to do better.

Chapter Twelve

I Am So Sorry

The whole way home on the school bus, Kenny didn't glance in my direction once. Now that it was all over, I felt as if a huge rock had been lifted off my chest. Paula and I told Ella, Yukiko, and Ariel all about our reports. For the thousandth time I wished that Jasmine could ride the school bus with us.

"So the Beast is pretty mad, huh?" asked Yukiko.

I nodded and sighed. "I'm going to have to apologize."

"You'll feel better once you do," Ella said.

"Why did Mr. Murchison keep him after class a few minutes?" Paula asked.

"I don't know," I said, feeling my brow crinkle up. "I expected him to keep *me* after class. I'm sure Kenny told him it was all my fault. I guess I'll probably get in trouble tomorrow."

"Maybe not," said Paula. "Maybe Murch will believe it was just a misunderstanding."

"Anyway, I'm glad this week is over," I said. "It's been a long one. The McIlhennys should be home tomorrow. I will never have to share a bathroom with the Beast again."

My friends laughed at me.

At home, Kenny rushed into my house and slammed the front door in my face. I opened it and followed him into the kitchen, where he flung his backpack onto the kitchen table. I set mine down. Through the kitchen window, we could see Mom tending her herb garden in the backyard. (I have my very own herb garden, too.)

Suddenly Kenny whirled on me. I had never seen him look so angry—not even the time I had smeared Vaseline all over the seat of his bicycle. (That was last year.)

"Ten pages!" he yelled, waving his arms. I blinked and took a step back. "All week you watched me killing myself, working like a maniac on *ten pages* of Orlando history!"

"Well, you got only seven done," I pointed out mildly.

He glared at me. "While I was *sick*! While I had a *fever*!"

I almost reminded him that he had a fever only on Monday and Tuesday of last week, but I stopped myself in time. He had every right to be angry. Even though he's a mean-spirited, small-minded, yucky boy who has done too many mean and sneaky things to me to even count, still. Even though he said awful things about me to his friends after my mom (and I) had taken care of him all week, even though I had been walking his humongous slobbery dog Otto for eight days—still, I knew I shouldn't have done what I did. No matter how much Kenny deserved it, I owed it to myself to be a better person than that. I had standards to live up to: Disney Girl standards, Beaumont standards, and finally, Halese's standards.

So I took a deep breath. "Kenny, I'm sorry," I burst in on his tirade. (He had just been getting warmed up.) "I know it was wrong to give you that fake assignment. And I actually did feel a little guilty all week, watching you slaving away."

"A *little* guilty! Gee, thanks!" Kenny said snidely. He wasn't going to make this easy on me by being gracious or anything.

"But every time I started to tell you," I plowed on, raising my voice, "you did something finky to me, or said something mean! Like just now! In fact, today I started to tell you about it before we even did the reports. But when I walked up behind you in the school yard, you were telling your dorky friends how ugly I was, and how awful it was living here! After all I've done for you this past week! You dweeb!" I practically yelled.

Kenny had been about to start yelling back, but he froze when he realized that I'd heard him today. His mouth opened and closed silently. His arms hung motionless in the air.

"Oh . . . " he said.

"My mom's been taking care of you! I've been bringing you drinks! I've been walking your dog!" I shouted.

Kenny held up a finger. "Hey, you *liked* walking Otto, once you started wearing your skates."

"That's not the point," I said. "My feelings were totally hurt today when I heard you say all that garbage. Who knows what you say about me when I *don't* overhear?"

71

Kenny looked sheepish. "I don't say mean things about you all the time," he muttered. "It was just, today, see, the guys were sort of teasing me about living here." His voice dropped to a mumble. "Like we were married or some- thing," he got out in a strangled whisper, turning away.

I gasped. "*Eww!* Gross!"

"I know," Kenny said. "I freaked. That's why I was say- ing all that stuff. To get them off my back. But I didn't, you know, mean for you to, you know, hear it. I, uh, guess I'm, you know, a little sorry I hurt your feelings."

I had to lean closer to him to hear the last part. It sounded an awful lot like an apology. And from the Beast! It was almost magical!

"Well, I'm sorry about the report," I said.

We stood there for a few moments, digesting every- thing. If this had been one of the DGs, we would have hugged to make up. But that was out of the question with Kenny.

Kenny shrugged. "Actually, it worked out okay," he admitted. "I had done so much extra work that Murch gave me extra credit, so it brought my grade up. Also, I'm going to be the Audio-Visual helper for the rest of the month."

My mouth dropped open when I realized that Kenny had been mad at me all afternoon, and had yelled at me, when, after all, I had actually done him a huge favor! I stared at him. Suddenly, I felt myself grinning. Kenny grinned back. The whole thing seemed ridiculous, and soon we were laughing so hard we had to sit down before we fell over.

I was pounding my fist on the kitchen table, trying to catch my breath, when I accidentally knocked my backpack over. That old zipper split, and all my books spilled out onto the floor. For some reason, this seemed like the funniest thing we had ever seen, and we started cackling all over again.

Gasping with laughter, I looked down to see my books and notebooks strewn across the kitchen floor. Then it hit me. I gulped and swallowed my laughter hard. I dropped to the floor and pawed through my stuff.

"Oh, no, Kenny!" I wailed. "It's gone! My ancestor's blouse is gone!"

Chapter Thirteen

Kenny to the Rescue

"What, that old shirt you were wearing for your report?" Kenny asked.

"That shirt was over a hundred years old!" I cried. "It was handmade! My mom is going to kill me!" I raced through the house and out the front door, hoping to see Halese's blouse lying in the grass somewhere. Nothing. I felt as if someone had punched me hard in the stomach. Mom was going to be so, so upset.

"That stupid zipper! I should have quit using that backpack last week!" I said. "I should have put the blouse

74

in a different bag! I should have gotten a ride to school today!"

"Wait—wait," said Kenny, holding up his hand. "Calm down. Look—maybe it fell out of your backpack at school, or on the school bus. I can call them and ask, okay?"

"Thank you, Kenny," I said, shocked. We went back inside my house. He went to the kitchen. I ran to my room, shut the door, and grabbed my magic mirror. (All of us DGs have magic charms that help us get in touch with our magic. Mine is a small silver mirror. Jasmine's is a tiny gold lamp. Ella's is a little crystal slipper. Paula's is a silver feather charm, and Yukiko's is a gold heart. Ariel's is, of course, a silver seashell.) I whispered:

"All the magic powers that be,
Hear me now, my special plea.
It's Belle, and you must help me see
Where dear Halese's blouse could be."

I closed my eyes for a second, then opened them and gazed into my mirror. At first it looked cloudy, as it always does, but then an image began to form. It was the blouse! I strained to make out its surroundings. It wasn't on a school bus. It wasn't in a classroom. It was lying by a bush somewhere. But where?

The image faded just as Kenny knocked on my door.

"Yes?" I opened it.

"It's not at school or on the bus," he reported in a whisper. (I already knew that.) "But I have an idea. Let's tell your mom we're taking Otto for a walk. Otto's a champion bloodhound, remember? He's trained to track scents."

My eyes almost popped out of my head. "Kenny!" I whispered. "That is so, so brilliant!"

Kenny looked pleased.

If you have never used a purebred champion bloodhound to track something, let me tell you: it is not as much fun as it sounds. It is even less fun than walking them, and you know how I feel about that.

"Come on, boy!" Kenny said, holding tightly to Otto's leash. He was letting Otto scent one of my T-shirts, which had been washed in the same detergent as the blouse.

"Do you really think this will work?" I asked.

"Hey, even though Otto's retired, he's still got one of the best noses in Orlando," said Kenny. "Probably."

It was the "probably" I was worried about.

Kenny and I snapped on our in-line skates, Kenny gave Otto the "track" command, and we were off!

It was like being dragged behind a crazed roller coaster. Otto pulled us forward, backward, in circles, through hedges, across fields (try it on your skates), and through mud puddles. I was losing hope fast.

"Wait a minute!" I panted when we got to the edge of Willow Green. I collapsed onto a bench. "I just need to regroup a minute."

Kenny collapsed next to me. "This is hard work," he said tiredly.

"I want you to know I appreciate your help," I said, "even if we don't find the blouse."

"You should have put it in another bag," Kenny said grumpily.

I almost smiled. Things were back to normal again.

"Hey! Isabelle!" I heard Jasmine yell. I looked up in surprise to see the five DGs running toward me!

"How did you guys know I'd be here?" I cried as they surrounded us.

"A little bird told me," said Jasmine, giving me a meaningful glance. "And I called everyone else. We're here to help you look for your blouse." That's one of the magical things about being a Disney Girl. The six of us are all so in tune with each other that we can often tell when one of us needs help.

"This is great," Kenny groaned. "If any of my friends see me surrounded by the Orlando glee club, I'll never live down the humiliation."

"Look, we have to work together," Paula directed. "Quick, group huddle."

We all stood up and formed a tight circle. I pulled Kenny in next to me. Under his breath he was muttering, "Please don't let anyone see me, please don't let anyone see me . . . "

All of us except Kenny closed our eyes. We murmured an almost silent secret wish to help me find my blouse. Then we opened our eyes.

Kenny's brown eyes narrowed. "What are you, some kind of cult?" he asked accusingly. "Hey!" Otto was yanking hard on his leash, almost pulling Kenny off his skates.

"Follow him!" Ella yelled.

The Beast and I rolled after Otto, almost out of control as he bounded across the field. The edge of Willow Green is bordered by Hapwell Street. I remembered the school bus driving down Hapwell on our way home.

"I see it!" I yelled, pointing to a crumpled lump of cream-colored cotton. Kenny got to the blouse just as Otto was about to seize it in his massive jaws. Quickly he snatched it up and held it over his head so Otto couldn't reach it.

Breathless, I skated up. Kenny held it out to me. I examined it all over. It looked okay!

"Oh, Kenny, thank you," I said happily. "You're a lifesaver!"

"As weird as that may be to believe," said Ariel darkly.

"Yeah, well, it was really Otto," Kenny said, embarrassed.

I bent down and hugged Otto's big head, slobber and all. "Thank you, Otto! I'll never say anything bad about you again!"

Chapter Fourteen

Easy Come, Easy Go

"I can't believe I hugged him for nothing!" Ariel cried, pounding her fist against the kitchen counter.

Paula and I grinned at each other. Yukiko's oldest little brother, Ben, passed through the kitchen.

"Who did you hug?" he asked with interest.

"Nobody," Ariel muttered. After Ben left, she pounded the counter again. "I hugged the Beast," she moaned. "Then I waited and waited. And my mom tells me yesterday that I'd already had chicken pox when I was a baby!"

"Hmm," Paula said, tapping her finger against her chin. "Ariel hugged Kenny. On purpose. Now, who could we tell about this?"

"You wouldn't dare!" Ariel shrieked.

Laughing, Yukiko set another bowl of dip on the counter. I looked around happily. Everything in my life was perfect. Kenny had been living back at his own house a week now. We had called a truce, for the time being. Who knew how long it would last? But it was fine for now.

My mom never knew that I had almost lost Halese's blouse for good. When I brought it home that day, we had taken it to a professional fabric restorer. That person had cleaned it, put preservatives on it, and then Mom and I had actually had it framed, as if it were a work of art. Now it hung in the hallway of our house.

As you know, Ariel never did catch the chicken pox. I'd always thought her plan was pretty silly.

Now it was Saturday night, and we were all at Yukiko's house for one of our famous Disney Girl sleepovers! Things are always a little crazed at Yukiko's house because of her six little brothers and one baby sister. Right now baby Suzie was cooing in her infant seat, looking so adorable as she played with her feet and smiled at us. I thought she looked like a plump little flower fairy. Us DGs were hanging out, eating chips and dip before we started tonight's film festival.

"You guys won't believe this," I said, "but I almost miss Otto."

"You're right," said Ella, dipping a chip. "I don't believe you."

"I mean, I don't miss his slobber or anything," I pointed out. "But he wasn't a bad dog. And Snuffles and Pokey adored him. You should have seen them all sleeping together."

"Next thing you know, you'll actually be missing Kenny," said Paula, snickering.

I swiped a chip in dip and lobbed it at Paula before I knew what I was doing. It landed with a wet plop on the counter in front of her.

Her dark eyes widened, and she aimed a carrot stick at my head.

"You guys, no food fights in the kitchen," Yukiko's step-dad, Jim, said sternly as he passed through the kitchen. "Take them outside."

Next thing I knew, I was running outside with my

friends, dodging carrots and chips and little boys and some mini pretzels. It was a warm and sunny evening, and the light made Yukiko's garden look like an enchanted place.

Sometimes it's good just to tell magic thanks.

So thanks.

It was the saddest Disney Girl sleepover ever. In fact, it was the only sad sleepover I could ever remember us having. I mean, that time Kenny McIlhenny taped us singing and dancing—well, that made us all furious. And the time four of Yukiko's little brothers had put itching powder in our sleeping bags—hat had been a big pain. And the time Isabelle's dad had told us we were all spending a week at Walt Disney World—that had been the absolute best sleepover! Now my five best friends and I were in the middle of an awful, terrible, horrible, bummingest Friday night. And it was all my fault.

"You have five seconds to tell us you're kidding," said Isabelle, my *best*, best friend.

"I'm not," I said miserably. "It's true. Mother thinks I'm old enough now to start at St. John's Academy."

"But it's in Virginia," Ella pointed out.

"I know. It's a boarding school," I said.

"Jasmine, you can't go away to boarding school," said Ariel firmly.

"Unless you pack us all up and take us with you." Her face brightened. "Hey! There's an idea."

"Forget it," I said glumly. "I'm going to St. John's next week, without all you guys, and that's it."

Then I burst into tears.

Read all the books in the
Disney Girls series!

#1 One of Us

Jasmine is thrilled to be a Disney Girl. It means she has four best friends—Ariel, Yukiko, Paula, and Ella. But she still doesn't have a *best* best friend. Then she meets Isabelle Beaumont, the new girl. Maybe Isabelle could be Jasmine's *best* best friend—but could she be a *Disney Girl*?

#2 Attack of the Beast

Isabelle's next-door neighbor Kenny has been a total Beast for as long as she can remember. But now he's gone too far: he secretly videotaped the Disney Girls singing and dancing and acting silly at Isabelle's slumber party. Isabelle vows to get the tape back, but how will she ever get past the Beast?

#3 And Sleepy Makes Seven

Mrs. Hayashi is expecting a baby soon, and Yukiko is praying that this time it'll be a girl. She's already got six younger brothers and stepbrothers, and this is her last chance for a sister. All of the Disney Girls are hoping that with a little magic, Yukiko's fondest wish will come true.

#4 A Fish Out of Water

Ariel in ballet class? That's like putting a fish in the middle of the desert! Even though Ariel's the star of her swim team, she decides that she wants to spend more time with the other Disney Girls. So she joins Jasmine and Yukiko's ballet class.

But has Ariel made a mistake, or will she trade in her flippers for toe shoes forever?

#5 *Cinderella's Castle*

The Disney Girls are so excited about the school's holiday party. Ella decides that the perfect thing for her to make is an elaborate gingerbread castle. But creating such a complicated confection isn't easy, even for someone as super-organized as Ella. And her stepfamily just doesn't seem to understand how important this is to her. Ella could really use a fairy godmother right now. . . .

#6 *One Pet Too Many*

Paula's always loved animals, any animal. Who else would have a pet raccoon, not to mention three cats, three dogs, four finches, and fish? When Paula finds a lost armadillo, though, her parents say, "No more pets!"—and that's that. But how much trouble could an armadillo be? Plenty, as Paula discovers—especially when she's trying to keep it a secret from her parents.

#7 *Adventure in Walt Disney World:*
A Disney Girls Super Special

The Disney Girls are so excited. The three pairs of *best* best friends are going to spend a week together at Walt Disney World. Find out how the Disney Girls' magical wishes come true as they have the adventure of their lives.

continued . . .

#8 *Beauty's Revenge*

Isabelle is thrilled when she finds out that her beastly neighbor, Kenny, will be going away on vacation for a week with his family. Then Kenny comes down with chicken pox—and he has to stay at Isabelle's house for the week! She might be tempted to feel bad for Kenny—if he wasn't being his usual beastly self. With the help of the Disney Girls and a little magic, she decides to give Kenny a taste of *her* own medicine.

#9 *Good-bye, Jasmine?*

Jasmine has always been a little bit different from the other Disney Girls. She lives in the wealthy Wildwood Estates instead of in Willow Hill like her friends. But at least the girls get to see each other every day at Orlando Elementary. Then one day Jasmine's mother decides that it's time for her daughter to attend her alma mater, St John's boarding school. The Disney Girls are in shock. Will they have to say good-bye to one of their best friends?